T0064571

ENTOMOVILLE

The city of insects

Nigel Shuford

authorHOUSE®

AuthorHouse™
1663 Liberty Drive
Bloomington, IN 47403
www.authorhouse.com
Phone: 1 (800) 839-8640

Published by AuthorHouse 06/22/2015

ISBN: 978-1-5049-1765-0 (sc)
ISBN: 978-1-5049-1766-7 (e)

Print information available on the last page.

This book is printed on acid-free paper.

CHAPTER 1

The Announcement

"Marcia, Marcia wake up", Ms. Jones shouted from down stairs.

"It's time to go to school", She said.

"Ok mama I'm awake", Marcia replied.

It was January in the year 2030. Marcia Jones is living in a strange surburban city called Trojan City.

"Remember to wear your winter coat when you get outside" Ms. Jones said.

"Yes mama, I will", Marcia replied.

Marcia is going back to school from her Christmas Vacation. Marcia was one of the smartest juniors in her junior year in John Smith Community Academy. She always wears her favorite Mickey Mouse glasses and her favorite red and black Nike gym shoes.

"I will wait for you in the car Marcia", Ms. Jones said, opening the front door in the house. "Just get out in ten minutes", She said.

So Marcia grabs her books and her school supplies and head outside to the car to go to school.

Arriving at school, all students in the Academy are waiting to get inside the building. Ms. Jones brought Marcia in front of the school's building while her friends, Pam, Mark, and Bobby were waiting outside for her. Pam Stevenson, who is always talking about everything that is going on in this city, is Marcia's best friend since middle school. Mark Brooks, the tough guy that does not fear anything, know Marcia since freshman year. Bobby Owens, who is always the quiet one, moved in the same neighborhood with Marcia since eighth grade. His family moved out of Africa from a devastating war.

"Hi! Everybody" Marcia said.

"Hey! Girlfriend" Pam replied.

"What's up Marcia?" Mark asked.

"How are you doing Marcia?" Bobby asked.

"So are you ready to go back to this boring class?" Mark asked.

"Yeah I'm ready to go to this boring and stupid class", Bobby said. "We have to be there in ten minutes", He said.

"Well we can be late going to class", Pam said. "So come on and let's do something fun", she said.

"No we can't, we might get in trouble if we get caught", Bobby said.

"Oh quick your complaining Owens", Mark said.

Suddenly the bell rings in John Smith Community

Academy. An officer from outside opened the doors and started shouting to the students.

"Okay students it's time to go to class", Officer Wayne Phillips shouted to the students.

So everyone went inside the Academy and gone to their classes. Marcia and her friends went to their first class Entomology 101.

Inside Entomology class, the teacher Mr. Nash greets everyone back to school.

"Welcome back students!" Mr. Nash said to the class. "I hope everyone had a great holiday break and I hope everyone read your chapters so let's continue on where we left off", He said.

Mr. Nash is one of the friendly teachers that anyone in the school can possibly have.

"Okay class, take out your book and turn to page 200 and we will study more about insects and how they survived", Mr. Nash said. "But before we begin I have an announcement to make", He said. "We are going to a field trip in two months", He said.

"Where are we going Mr. Nash?" Marcia said.

"Well, we are going to Pesticide Corporation", Mr. Nash replied.

"Awwwwwwww Maaaaaannnnnnn!" The whole class shouted.

"We are going to Pesticide Corporation to learn more about insects and we are going on March 12th and everyone will be pair up so we don't have to lose anyone during the trip", Mr. Nash said. "So with that, read page 200 silently while I take attendance", He said.

So class begins and everyone is silently reading.

Before class ended, Mr. Nash starts to pass out permission slips for the field trip and dismisses the students.

"Have a nice day everyone and continue to read page 200 because it might assign you guys a pop quiz", He said.

So everyone has left the classroom and headed for their lockers. Marcia and her friends started to talk about the trip.

"So are you guys going to Pesticide Corporation?" Marcia asked.

"I guess so", Pam replied.

"I guess we can learn something from Pesticide Corporation", Bobby said.

"Right, it may help us get a passing grade from the class", Marcia said.

"So you'll think that this stupid company can help us pass this class?" Mark asked. "Well, I'm not going anywhere except going home", He said.

"Come on tough guy, go with us for once", Bobby said.

"Please!!!!" Pam begged.

"If you go with us, I'll let you keep the new Nascar game for the Playstation 2000 that came out just a few weeks ago", Bobby said.

"It's a deal Bobby Owens", Mark said.

"All right, I see you guys later", Marcia said.

"Good bye Marcia", Pam said.

So Marcia and her friends went home to prepare for another day.

CHAPTER 2

The Secret Laboratory

The next day the phone rings in Marcia's house.

"Hello!" Ms. Jones answered.

"Hi Ms. Jones, may I speak to Marcia please?" Pam asked.

"Yes, hold on please", Ms. Jones replied.

"Marcia, your friend Pam is on the phone", She shouted.

"Ok Mom!" Marcia shouted from upstairs.

Marcia starts running down the stairs and pick up the phone.

"Hi! Pam", Marcia said.

"Hey Marcia, are you going to Pesticide Corporation?" Pam asked.

"Yes, I will be there", Marcia said.

"Did you call Mark and Bobby?" Marcia asked.

"Yes I did", Pam answered.

"We will arrive at the school in fifteen minutes", She said.

"Ok, I will see you there", Marcia said.

Marcia hangs up the phone and prepare for a field trip.

Arriving at school, Marcia sees her friends in front of the bus stop.

"So, are you guys ready for this boring trip?" Marcia asked to her friends.

"Of course I am", Bobby said.

"I do not know why you are excited", Mark said.

"Hey, I think this trip will be interesting", Bobby said.

"I think so too", Marcia said.

The city bus has just arrived and the kids enter the bus. Ten minutes later, they have arrived at the school and walk towards Entomology 101 classroom. Mr. Nash has just arrived in the classroom and put his books on his desk.

"Hi Mr. Nash", Pam said.

"Well hello Pam, are you ready for an exciting trip in your life", Mr. Nash asked.

"Oh yes Mr. Nash", Pam said.

"All right class, please give me your permission slips to me so I can turn them in to the principal and we can get this show on the road", Mr. Nash said.

"Now, the bus will arrive in ten minutes so be prepared for it", He said.

So the kids in the classroom room gave the permission slips to Mr. Nash. Mark turns around for his desk and begins to talk to Pam.

"Hey Pam, were you serious about the trip?" Mark asked.

"No, I was trying to impress him", Pam said.

"You like Mr. Nash?" Marcia asked.

"No, I was just kidding", Pam said, with blush on her face.

Ten minutes later, the bus has arrived. Everyone leaves the classroom and headed outside towards the bus. They have line up in front of the bus and waited to be seated.

"Ok everyone, I want four people in a group so we don't get lost", Mr. Nash said. So everyone paired up into groups and sat down on the bus. The bus left the school and headed towards Pesticide Corporation. The time is 9:30a.m. and the students has just arrived to Pesticide Corporation. All of the students are in their groups and of course, Marcia and her friends always pair up.

As the students arrive at the building, one of the tour guides, Ms. Parks has walk towards the students.

"Well this might be the students from John Smith Academy, how are you students", Ms. Parks said, with a big smile on her face. "Welcome to Pesticide Corporation and I hope everyone had a wonderful morning", She said.

"Class, this is Ms. Parks and she will be our tour guide for today", Mr. Nash said.

"Thank You Mr. Nash", Ms. Parks said. "Well class let's begin our tour", She said.

So Ms. Parks begins to give the class a tour of Pesticide Corporation. While Ms. Parks give the class the tour to the company, Marcia and her friends escape the tour and begin their own exploring to the company.

"Hey over here", Pam whispered. "What's over there?" She asked.

"It's a door that says, "DO NOT ENTER", Bobby said.

"Let's go over there", Mark said.

"No way, we'll get in trouble if we go there", Bobby said.

"Oh be quiet Bobby, I say let's go there", Mark said.

"Maybe Mark's right", Marcia said. "I think we should spice things up from this trip and have ourselves a little adventure", She said.

"I agree, let's do this", Pam said.

So Marcia and her friends decided to open the "DO NOT ENTER" door and went inside. There were no security guards in site or no people watching over them. When they got inside the room, they saw something strange.

"What is this place?" Bobby asked, entering the room.

"This place look like a laboratory", Pam said.

"Why would a huge company like Pesticide would keep a place like this?" Marcia asked.

"Maybe they keeping a secret experiment over here", Bobby said.

"Could be" Pam wondered.

"Hey, I found something", Mark whispered.

Mark has found a bee inside of a small tube of water.

"Oh my god, why would they have a bee in the water", Pam said.

"Plus its dead", Marcia said.

"What's going on here?" Bobby asked.

"Look, I found something else", Mark said.

Mark has found more insects like wasps and flies inside of a little tube of water.

"I think they are doing some type of experiment to these insects", Bobby said.

"I say let's break the tube and ruin this laboratory", Mark said.

"No we can't", Pam said.

"She's right", Bobby said.

"Relax Owens, no one will find out", Mark said.

"No we have to get out of here before we get caught", Marcia said.

"That's a good idea", Pam said. "Come on, let's go", She said.

Suddenly the tubes were shaking and the entire insects bust out of their tubes and escaped.

"Oh my god, what just happen?" Pam shouted with fear.

"I thought these things were dead", Mark said.

The insects were flying around the laboratory and the kids stood still in one spot.

"DO NOT PANIC", Marcia said. "If we stood still they would not mess with us", She said.

But Mark moved backwards and bumps into a bigger tube in the laboratory. He turns around slowly and trembling with fear.

"Hey guys, what is this?" Mark asked, shaking with fear.

Mark found a strange man sleeping inside of a big tube full of water.

"Now what's really going on here?" Bobby wondered.

This man inside the tube was tall, half-naked with only wearing his underwear, and has claws as his hands.

"This man is ugly", Pam said.

"Hey, let's release him", Pam said.

"No way, he might attack us", Bobby said.

"Well, I'm going to release him", Mark said.

"It's too many buttons and controls", Marcia said.

"Just press anything", Mark said.

But before Marcia even touches anything, the man eyes opened.

"Oh my god, HE'S ALIVE", Pam shouted.

"Hello can you hear me", Bobby asked to the man in the tube.

But the strange man did not say anything.

"Ok this place is started to freak me out", Marcia said.

"Let's get out of here before anything else goes wrong", Bobby said.

"Agree, let's go", Pam said.

But before everyone is ready to leave the laboratory, the strange man breaks through the glass with his claws.

"LOOK OUT!" Bobby shouted. "Let's get out of here", He shouted, running towards the door.

The kids escape the laboratory and everyone in Pesticide

Corporation pause and looking at the frighten kids including the students in John Smith Academy.

"Hey you kids, what are you doing over there?" said the security guard, looking at the kids escaping the laboratory. "This is a restricted area", He said.

"Marcia, Pam, Bobby, and Mark, I have told you guys to stay together", Mr. Nash said with anger.

"But we saw insects and a real man inside", Pam said to Mr. Nash.

"Oh really, well we'll see about this", the security guard said.

The security guard went inside the laboratory but when he went inside, there was no man inside except for insects flying around.

"Did you break something?" the security guard said to the kids. "Those insects were part of a good experiment that scientists in this company are working on", He said.

"But we saw a strange man inside of a giant tube", Pam said.

THAT'S ENOUGH!" Mr. Nash shouted.

"But we saw him Mr. Nash honest", Bobby said.

"No more excuses", Mr. Nash said. "You four are going to detention for three weeks", He said.

"Sorry about that sir", Mr. Nash said to the security guard.

"That's ok", the security guard said.

"All right class, let's headed back to the bus and go back to school", Mr. Nash said.

So the class headed back to the bus and went back to school. Marcia and her friends couldn't believe what has happen and they were surprise that no one; didn't believe them.

CHAPTER 3

Terror at Pesticide Corporation

Marcia and the gang enjoy their weekend after the field trip. They went to the mall to buy clothes and video games.

Hey, the new fighting game comes out today", Mark said to Bobby, walking towards a video game store.

"What's the name of the game?" Bobby asked.

"It's called *Chaos Fighting*", Mark said. "The game has thirty characters and five hidden characters", He said.

Marcia and Pam were in the clothing store buying new clothes.

"Hey Marcia, check out this new dress", Pam said, pulling out the new dress from the clothes rack.

The dress was black, with a flower on the upper right of the dress's sleeve.

"How much is the dress Pam?" Marcia asked.

"The dress is only fifty dollars", Pam said.

"Well I have to save my money to buy this", Marcia said.

"OK!" Pam said.

So Marcia and her friends continue to shop at the mall.

Meanwhile, nighttime has come at Pesticide Corporation. The lights are turn off and the only people that is working are two officers of the law.

"Everything is clear on the first floor", Officer Jenkins said, talking on his walkie-talkie.

"Everything is secure in the second floor", Officer Bennett responded.

Both of the security guards went back to the monitor room and watch over Pesticide Corporation through the monitors.

"I'm going to take a nap", Officer Jenkins said.

"Ok, I guess I'll watch over Pesticide", Officer Bennett said. "But, it's your turn next", He said.

"Fine, I'll do it", Officer Jenkins said.

Pesticide Corporation is very quiet and all of the insects in the exhibitions were quiet as well.

Ten minutes later, a crash was heard at Pesticide Corporation.

"What was that?" said Officer Jenkins, waking up from his nap.

"Maybe we need to check it out", Officer Bennett said.

"Look, the monitor shows that the crash coming from the secret laboratory on the first floor", Officer Jenkins said.

So both security guards went to the secret laboratory to see what has happened. Officer Jenkins opened the door and when he peeks inside, a strange man jumps out of the lab and attack him.

"Ahhhhhh! Get this creature off me", Officer Jenkins yelled, struggling to get the strange man off him. The strange man was biting Officer Jenkins neck like he was a zombie. Officer Bennett pulls out a gun and fire at the strange man. The strange man was down but Officer Jenkins did not move.

"Hey, get up", Officer Bennett said.

Officer Jenkins still did not move. While Officer Bennett tries to get his partner to get up, the strange man slowly gets up off the floor and started to moan.

Officer Bennett turns around and saw the strange man got up off the floor.

"Oh my god, he's still alive", Officer Bennett shouted with fear.

The strange man walks towards Officer Bennett and opened his mouth.

"Dude, your breath stink", said Officer Bennett, smelling the strange man breath.

But the strange man did not open his mouth to let Officer Bennett smell his breath, there were wasps and flies swirling around inside of his mouth. The wasps and flies came out of the strange man's mouth and attack Officer Bennett.

"AHHHHHH! Get off me", Officer Bennett yelling and swinging his arms around trying to get the wasps and flies off him.

The wasps and flies were eating Officer Bennett's skin

and sucking his blood. Officer Jenkins got up off the floor and jumps on Officer Bennett and starts to bite his neck with his long teeth.

"AHHHHHHH!" Officer Bennett yelled, being eating by his partner and the insects.

The only thing that was left from Officer Bennett was his human skeleton. The strange man and Officer Bennett had walked away. Wasps and flies were still swarming around at Officer Bennett.

The next morning, an employee from Pesticide Corporation named Sarah Cook walks inside the company. She went to the breaker room to turn the lights on. She walks around the whole building to unlock all of the doors. But when she unlocks the secret laboratory, she saw Officer Bennett lying on the floor dead.

"Oh my god, he's dead", Sarah shouted, covering her mouth with her hands.

She went to the nearest phone and quickly calls the police.

"911 what's your emergency?" the operator on the phone said.

"Hello, there is a man dead on the ground with no skin on his face", Sarah said with fear.

"Ok, what is your location ma'am?" the operator said.

"I am in Pesticide Corporation at 4621 Brooks street", Sarah said.

"Ok the police will arrive in ten minutes", the operator said.

Meanwhile at John Smith Community Academy, Marcia and her friends were in detention. The teacher Mr. Watson decides to turn on the T.V and watch the news.

"Hey check it out, the news is on", Pam said to her friends.

"We have breaking news in Pesticide Corporation that an officer has been found dead in a laboratory", the news reporter said. "The police said that Sarah Cook, an employee who works for the company found the officer on the ground with no skin in his face, seems that the man was eaten alive", She said.

"Oh wow, an officer was killed", Bobby said.

"The security guard had no skin", Marcia said.

"He was dead at the laboratory", Mark said.

"Maybe it was that man that we saw at the laboratory", Pam said.

"You could be right Pam" Marcia said.

"I think we should go there and investigate the situation", Mark said.

"Good idea Mark", Pam said.

"But we have to get out of here first", Bobby said.

"All right you guys, stop talking and get back to work", Mr. Watson shouted.

So Marcia and her friends continue to do their homework and serve their time in the detention.

CHAPTER 4

Investigating Pesticide

After the detention, Marcia and her friends are walking in the hallway to talk about the breaking news that happened in Pesticide Corporation.

"Hey did you hear? Pesticide is closed until the investigation is over", Marcia said to her friends.

"What investigation?" Bobby asked Marcia.

"The police are investigating the incident that happened last night", Marcia said.

"Hey, maybe we should check it out on our own", Mark said.

"But how are we supposed to get inside without permission?" Bobby asked.

"Relax Bobby, all we have to do is to tell our parents that we are going to Pesticide Corporation to do some community service hours", Mark said.

"I think that's a great idea", Pam said.

"Well ok, we have to call our parents right away", Marcia said.

So Marcia and her friends call their parents on their cell phones to tell them that they are going to Pesticide Corporation for community service.

After Marcia and her friends call their parents and told them about doing community service hours for Pesticide, they took the bus to Pesticide Corporation. When they got there, there were a lot of police vehicles park in the parking lot.

"How are we going to get inside?" Pam asked.

"Easy Pam, just sneak inside and get past the police officers", Mark explained.

"But what if we get caught?" Bobby asked.

"We are not going to get caught because we are too fast for them", Mark said.

"Mark you're silly", Pam said.

"How about we go around the back?" Marcia asked.

"Now that's a great idea", Bobby said.

Bobby went around the back to check to see were there any police officers in the back. While he was there, he saw a window that is crack open.

"Hey, there is a window that is opened", Bobby said.

"That's perfect, let's use the window to get inside", Marcia said.

"That's better than Mark's plan", Pam said.

"So what", Mark said.

So Marcia and her friends sneak around the back and use the window to get inside the building. While they were inside, a lot of flashlights were flashing in Pesticide Corporation.

"Oh great, we're trap like rats", Bobby said.

"Now what Marcia?" Mark asked.

"Don't worry Mark, we will figure out a way to get inside the secret laboratory without getting caught", Marcia said.

"How about hiding under that desk over there?" Pam asked, pointing at a big black desk at the center of Pesticide.

Great idea Pam", Marcia said.

So Marcia and her friends hide under a big black desk.

They waited and waited and thirty minutes later, the police officers left the building.

"Well I guess there is no monsters around", said Chief Skinner, leaving Pesticide Corporation.

All of the police officers left the Pesticide Corporation and continue the investigating another day. Marcia and her friends were still hiding under the big black desk.

"Good, the close is clear", said Pam, getting up off the floor.

"Now, let's do our own investigating", Mark said.

So Marcia and her friends went back to the secret laboratory to figure out the disaster happened last night.

"Wow, it's a lot of broken glass over here", said Bobby, walking towards the secret laboratory.

"Plus, it's too many bugs flying around", Pam said.

"We can't back down yet", Mark said.

"Right, we have to find out who cause this mess", Bobby said.

So Marcia and her friends continue to search for clues.

"Hey, look what I found", Mark said.

"It's a security badge", Pam said.

Mark found a security badge right next to the broken tube.

"Hey, there is that same tube we saw with that strange man", said Marcia, pointing at the broken tube.

"Maybe that strange man escaped", Bobby said.

"He must be hiding somewhere", Pam said.

Suddenly a moan sound was heard.

"What was that sound?" Mark asked.

"IT'S GETTING CLOSER", Pam shouted with fear.

The sound is getting closer and closer.

"We have to get out of here", Marcia said.

"But we can't back down now", Mark said.

Suddenly the strange man walked slowly behind Mark.

"MARK LOOK BEHIND YOU", Pam shouted.

Mark quickly roll out of the way and landed on a broomstick.

"Take this you monster", mark shouted with courage.

Mark hit the strange man with a broomstick on his head.

"Get him Mark", Bobby said.

But the broomstick did not faze him.

"It didn't work", Pam said.

"Now what", Marcia said.

The strange man shook off the pain, open his mouth, and flies and wasps came right out his mouth. The flies and the wasps went right into Mark's face.

"AHHHHHH, get these things off me", Mark shouted, wiping his face to get the flies and the wasps off me.

"Mark, just hang on", Bobby said.

"Here use this", Marcia said.

Marcia splashes some water on Mark's face. The flies and the wasps went away.

"Man, that's was a close one", Bobby said.

"Come on, let's get out of here quickly before someone shows up", Marcia said.

"Agree, let's go", Bobby said.

Suddenly two scientists came right in front of them and block their exit.

"What are you kids doing here?" said Dr. Splatter, the Executive Vice President of Pesticide Corporation

We cannot allow you to go any further", Dr. Miles said.

CHAPTER 5

Pesticide's Secret Plan

Dr. Splatter and his assistant, Allen Miles had a white jacket and wear two dress shoes.

"Why are you trespassing in my lab?" Dr. Splatter asked the kids.

"Who are you?" Pam asked.

"I am Dr. Joe Splatter and this is my assistant Dr. Allen Miles and we are in charge of this laboratory", Dr. Splatter said.

"Hi I'm Marcia and these are my friends", Marcia said, shaking Dr. Splatter's hand. "This is Bobby, Mark and Pam", She said, introducing her friends to Dr. Splatter.

"But you did not answer his question", Dr. Miles said.

"We won't answer your question until you answer ours", Mark said.

"And what's that if I must asked", Dr. Splatter said.

"What is that thing right there?" Mark asked, pointing at the strange man.

"That is our finest creation", Dr. Splatter said.

"That is a Humasect", Dr. Miles said.

"A Humasect…..What is a Humasect?" Pam asked.

"A Humasect is a half-human and a half-insect", Dr. Splatter replied. "Me and Dr. Miles create this creature for our future plans", He said.

"Future plans? Bobby wondered. "What is your future plan?" He asked.

"To create our own world full of insects", Dr. Miles said.

"We will be the new masers of this planet", Dr. Splatter said.

"Well, we here to stop you", Pam said.

"Oh Really!" Dr. Splatter said. "There is nothing you kids can do about it", He said.

"You kids are stuck here for life", Dr. Miles said.

"Well, I'm getting out of here", Mark said, walking towards the exit.

"No one is going anywhere", Dr. Splatter said, pulling a gun out of his jacket.

Marcia and her friends are shaking with fear. The kids are so shock that they didn't move.

"What are we going to do now?" Marcia asked to her friends.

"I don't know", Bobby said.

"SILENCE!!!!!" Dr. Miles shouted. "You kids know too much", He said.

"I think it's about time to begin our plan Miles", Dr. Splatter said to Dr. Miles

"Yes, let's do it", Dr. Miles responded. "But let's make sure these kids doesn't tell the police", He said.

"Hey Humasect, GET THEM", Dr. Miles order the Humasect to capture the kids.

The Humasect begins to chase the kids around Pesticide Corporation. The Humasect got enormous speed.

"This creature is gaining on us", said Pam, running to escape the Humasect.

"Hey guys, let's split up", Marcia said.

So Marcia and her friends split up to run from the Humasect.

"Hey Miles, sent another Humasect out there", Dr. Splatter said to Dr. Miles.

"Yes sir", Dr. Miles responded.

Miles press a button in the remote control and a big tube came under the laboratory. Inside the tube lays another Humasect and ran out of the lab.

"Hey Humasect, capture those kids over there", Dr. Miles said to the Humasect, pointing in the direction where the kids is being chase by a Humasect.

So the Humasect is out of the lab and begin chasing the kids.

"LOOK OUT!!!!" Pam shouted.

The Humasect that was out of the lab capture Mark and Pam from behind.

"NOOOOOOOOOOOOOO!!!!" Marcia shouted.

"LET THEM GO YOU BASTARD", Bobby shouted.

"There is nothing you can't do", Dr. Splatter said.

"Let me go NOW", Pam shouted; struggle to get away from the Humasect.

Suddenly the other Humasect is sneaking right behind Marcia and Bobby.

"LOOK OUT!!!!" Pam shouted.

The Humasect had capture Marcia and Bobby from behind.

"LET GO", Marcia shouted, struggling to get away from the Humasect.

"Excellent!" Dr. Splatter said. "Now, we can begin with our plan", He said.

"But first, we must make more Humasects", Dr. Miles said.

"Agree!" Dr. Splatter said.

"But wait, let's lock up these kids in the cage and place them with my newest creation", Dr. Splatter said.

"And what's that Splatter"? Mark asked.

"It's the Humbugizer", Dr. Splatter said. "The Humbugizer can change anyone into a Humasect without getting bitten", He explained.

"My Humasects, take them in the basement so we can begin our plan", He said.

So the Humasects took the kids in the basement under the secret laboratory.

"All right Miles, let's go", Dr. Splatter said.

CHAPTER 6

Secret Lab Destruction

Dr. Splatter kidnaps the kids and lock them in the cage. Dr. Splatter and Dr. Miles were in the basement under the secret lab. The basement is full of bugs connect with electric wires and Humasects are in a big tube full of water.

"Welcome to my basement", said Dr. Splatter, entering his basement.

"How would you keep all of this in your basement?" asked Pam, lock up in the cage.

"Easy my fair lady", Dr. Splatter said. "I told my fellow employees that I will use this basement for an important experiment", He said.

"You stupid lair", Mark said.

"Oh no, I am not a lair", Dr. Splatter said. "I am very loyalty", He said.

"Sir, we have to prepare the Humbugizer", Dr. Miles said.

"All right, let's do it", Dr. Splatter said.

So Dr. Splatter and his assistant Dr. Miles prepare the Humbugizer.

"It's time to send these kids to the Humbugizer", Dr. Splatter said.

"Yes, we will place bugs inside the Humbugizer with you kids in it", Dr. Miles said.

"The Humbugizer will transmit the bugs inside of your body", Dr. Splatter said.

"The bugs will travel all around your body including your brain and spread poison that will transform you into a Humasect", Dr. Miles explain to the kids.

"I will not be part of your stupid creation", said Mark, lock up in the cage.

"You stupid boy, you do not have a choice", Dr. Splatter said. "After we turn you kids into Humasects, we will begin part one of our plan", He said.

"What's that?" Bobby asked.

"Take the key from Mayor Jones and take over the city", Dr. Miles said.

"This key has the power to do anything in the city", Dr. Splatter said. "Now, it's time to put you kids inside the Humbugizer", He said.

The kids were trapped. They could not do anything.

"What are we going to do?" Bobby asked.

"I have a plan", Mark whispered.

"Quickly, what's the plan?" Marcia asked.

"We pretend we are dead", Mark said.

"That's a stupid plan Mark", Bobby said.

"Wait Bobby, I think that's a great idea", Marcia said.

"Yeah!" Pam said.

"Ok let's do it", Mark said.

So the kids pretend that they are dead. Marcia and her friends were lay out.

"What happen here?" Dr. Splatter asked, seeing the kids lay out.

"Maybe they got poison by the Humasects", Dr. Miles said.

"Nonsense, the Humasects couldn't open the cage", Dr. Splatter said.

"Now what sir", Dr. Miles said.

"Do not worry Miles", Dr. Splatter said. "We will take the Humasects to the city and take over the city", He said.

"All right, let's do it", Dr. Miles said.

So Dr. Splatter and his assistant Dr. Miles left the secret lab with two Humasects and on their way to Triad City. Meanwhile back in the lab, Marcia and her friends were still lock up in the cage in the secret laboratory and pretend to be dead.

"Hey, I think the coast is clear", Bobby said, waking up from his sleep.

"Where is Dr. Splatter?" Marcia asked.

"I heard he and his assistant is going to Triad City along with their Humasects", Pam said.

"That's right, they going to take the key from Mayor Jones and take over the city", Mark said.

"We have to get out of here", Marcia said.

"How?" Pam asked.

"I have a plan", Bobby said.

"What's that?" Mark asked.

"All we have to do is get a rock and hit the Humbugizer and the Humbugizer will knock down and break the bars in the cage", Bobby explained.

"Bobby that is the stupidest plan that I ever heard", Mark said.

"No mark, that's a great idea", Marcia said. "There is no other way we can get out besides having something to break out of this cage", She said.

"Look I found a rock", Pam said.

Pam found a big rock behind them in the cage.

"Good, I hope this works" Bobby said.

So Bobby grabs the rock and threw it to the Humbugizer. The Humbugizer did not knock over to break the bars in the cage. Instead, the Humbugizer was destroyed and causes a big explosion. The kids were trapped. The big explosion causes the secret laboratory to fall apart. Pieces of the ceiling begin to tremble down. The fire from the big explosion came closer and closer to the kids.

"We're trapped", Pam shouted, trap in the cage.

"Nice going Owens", Mark said.

"What are we going to do now?" Bobby asked.

"Well, you got us in this mess", Mark said. "Now, you have to get us out", He said.

The fire grew closer and closer to the kids.

"DO SOMETHING", Mark shouted, scare of the fire that was getting closer to him.

Luckily, the sprinklers from the ceiling came on and wash away the fire. But the secret laboratory was destroyed and the kids were still lock up in the cage.

"That was too close", Marcia said, still lock up in the cage. "I can't believe that we're still here", She said.

"There is nothing we can do", Bobby said.

"Bobby, let me handle the plans around here", Mark said.

"What was your plan Mark?" Bobby asked.

"Use the big rock to break the bars", Mark said.

"I don't think it will work", Pam said.

"Well we would probably try", Marcia said. "Now we stuck here", She said.

"Yeah, Dr. Splatter and Dr. Miles will take over the city and probably the world and it is my entire fault", Bobby said.

"Don't say that Bobby", Marcia said. "Let's just wait here until the police get here", She said.

So the kids fall asleep in the cage and hope someone rescue them.

CHAPTER 7

Splatter's Hostile Takeover

Meanwhile in Triad City, it was 9:00p.m. and people are leaving from work to go to their homes. The mayor, Steven Jones stays in his office and work for a few hours. His assistant, Mariah Cook is staying in the office to work with him. Dr. Splatter and Dr. Miles just arrive in the city with their Humasects.

"All right my Humasects, kill anyone that's gets in your way", Dr. Splatter said.

"After that, we will find the mayor's office and make him give us the key to the city", Dr. Miles said.

"Then, we will make this city of our own and travel to another city and another city until the world is ours HA HA HA HA HA", Dr. Splatter said, laughing with anger. "Now, let's move on with our plan", He said.

The Humasects and the two scientists look around the city. The city was crowded with people walking around and vehicles driving into their location.

"All right you guys, we will split up", Dr. Splatter said. "Me and Dr. Miles will find the mayor's office and you Humasects will kill everyone in sight", He said.

So Dr. Splatter and Dr. Miles went on to search the mayor's office in the city. The Humasects went out and kill two different people in the city. One of the Humasects kills a homeless person right next to a corner store. After that, the homeless person woke up as a Humasect. The other Humasect kills a lady while she was walking to her car. The lady woke up as a Humasect seconds later. The two Humasects continue to kill everyone in the city.

Meanwhile Dr. Splatter and Dr. Miles have found the mayor's office.

"This is it", Dr. Splatter said, walking towards the office.

"Yes, we found it at last", Dr. Miles said.

The two Humasects came back with more Humasects.

"Perfect, it's time to enter the office", Dr. Splatter said.

So Dr. Splatter and Dr. Miles with the Humasects enter the office. While inside, they met a security guard.

"How can I help you sir", Officer Anderson said to Dr. Splatter.

"Yes we need to speak to Mayor Steven Jones please", Dr. Splatter said.

"Sorry, he wish not to speak to anyone", Officer Anderson said.

"Well, we need to talk to him or else", Dr. Miles said.

"Are you threatening me?" Officer Anderson asked.

"Look, we are asking you to get out of the way or there will be some consequences from your actions", Dr. Miles said.

"GUARDS!!!!" Officer Anderson shouted.

More security guards come running out of the office to stop Dr. Splatter and Dr. Miles.

"HUMASECTS, DESTROY THEM", Dr. Splatter shouted.

The Humasects strikes at the security guards and kills them. During the war with Humasects and the security guards, Dr. Splatter and Dr. Miles enter the office.

Inside the office, the mayor's assistant, Mariah Cook is sitting right next to a door where the mayor's office is behind it.

"Hi, can I help you with something?" Mariah asked.

"Yes, where is the mayor?" Dr. Splatter asks Mariah.

"He is busy right now", Mariah said.

"Well, I guess we have to walk right in if you don't mind", Dr. Miles said.

"I can't let you do that", said Mariah, stepping right in front of the two scientists.

Suddenly Dr. Splatter strikes Mariah with a needle of venom in her arm.

"OUCH!!!! WHAT WAS THAT?" Mariah shouted.

"It is something special I have created", Dr. Splatter said.

"I still can not allow you to see him", Mariah said.

Suddenly Mariah is holding her stomach like something went wrong.

"AAAAAHHHHH, what's happening to me?" Mariah said, on the ground holding her stomach.

"Hey, what's going on here?" Mayor Jones asked, coming out of his office. "What happen to Ms. Cook?" He asked.

"Oh hello mayor, I'm Dr. Splatter and this is my assistant Dr. Miles and we are here to talk to you", Dr. Splatter said.

"I don't have time to talk to you", Mayor Jones said.

"Oh yes you do", Dr. Miles said. "There is a key that you have and we need that to take control of the city", He said.

"The key does not belong to anybody other than myself", Mayor Jones said.

"Well, I guess we have to take it by force", Dr. Splatter said.

"Get out of here before I call the police", Mayor Jones said.

"Hey Humasect, come here", Dr. Miles said.

One of the Humasects came to the office. "Destroy the office", Dr. Miles said.

"No stop it", Mayor Jones shouted, as the Humasect continue to destroy the office.

"Well Mayor Jones, do we have a deal", Dr. Splatter said.

"NO DEAL", Mayor Jones shouted.

"Oh well, I guess I don't have a choice", Dr. Splatter said. "HUMASECT ATTACK", He shouted.

The Humasect strikes the mayor with his claws and knock him out.

"Good, he's gone", Dr. Miles said.

"Now, let's find that key", Dr. Splatter said.

So Dr. Splatter and Dr. Miles search for the key inside the office. Meanwhile at the front of the office, Mariah Cook, who was struck at Dr. Splatter's needle started to change. Her heart was pumping fast, her skin was fading away, and her hair begins to fall on the ground. Suddenly she changes into a giant wasp with huge wings and a big needle in her butt.

Meanwhile back in the mayor's office, Dr. Splatter and his assistant had found the key to the city.

"Yes, this is it", Dr. Miles said.

The key was located inside a crack safe inside the mayor's office.

"Excellent, now we will begin our next plan", Dr. Splatter said.

"Yes, it is time to take over the city and then the world", Dr. Miles said. "But first, I have to do something", He said.

Dr. Miles went towards the mayor who was knock out by a Humasect and struck him with a needle full of venom.

"Ok, that's should do it", He said.

When they got out of the office, they saw Mariah Cook, who has turn into a giant wasp flying around outside the office.

"Hey my venom works", Dr. Splatter said.

"Is that Ms. Cook?" Dr. Miles asked.

"Yes, but we have to get out of here", Dr. Splatter said.

The two scientists begin to walk out of the office until Ms. Cook, who is a giant wasp charge both of the scientists with her poison needle.

"LOOK OUT!" Dr. Splatter shouted.

They roll out of the way and ran out of the office.

"Aw man, that was a close one", Dr. Miles said, catching his breath from running.

"Don't worry, we still have the key and now it's time to take over the city", Dr. Splatter said.

Ok now what boss", Dr. Miles said.

"Well, with this key we can do anything in the city", Dr. Splatter said. "So, let's do something fun", He said.

"Since we have the key, we can change the name and call it whatever we want", Dr. Miles said.

"Yes for now on, this city will be named "ENTOMOVILLE", Dr. Splatter shouted.

"But we need to find a hideout", Dr. Miles said.

"We can hide at the Triad Palace and that's where we will finish our experiments", Dr. Splatter said.

So Dr. Splatter and Dr. Miles leave the office to go to the Triad Palace. The city that's which was called Triad City is now change to Entomoville.

CHAPTER 8

Entomoville

Two years has passed and the city was nothing but flies and bees flying everywhere in the city. There were a lot of Humasects walking around looking for food but Dr. Splatter and Dr. Miles could not be found. Meanwhile back at the old laboratory, Marcia and her friends was still trap in the cage but they were sleeping. Ten minutes later, Marcia woke up from her sleep.

"Hey guys, wake up", said Marcia, waking up from her sleep.

"Are we still here?" Bobby asked.

"I guess so", Pam said.

"Where are Dr. Splatter and Dr. Miles?" Mark asked.

"I think they should be in the city", Marcia said.

"Well we have to get out of here before it's too late", Pam said.

"It's probably too late already", Bobby said.

"We need to try to get out of here fast like right now", Mark said.

"Yes, let's think of something so we can get out of here" Marcia said.

So the kids try to think of a plan to get out of the cage.

"I have a better plan", Mark said.

"What's that?" Pam asked.

"All we have to do is kick the door down", Mark said.

"The door is metal and that will never work", Bobby said.

"Well we just have to work together", Mark said.

"I think that's a great idea", Marcia said. "So let's try it", She said.

So the kids begin to kick the door down together.

"All right guys, we will kick the door on three", Bobby said.

"One…two….three", the kids shouted and start to kicking the door.

The kids repeatedly kick the door. Five minutes later, the door was finally opened.

"Finally, we are out of here", said Mark, celebrating with joy.

"Free at last", Pam said.

"Come on, we have to get of here and go to the city", Marcia said. "Dr. Splatter and Dr. Miles is already there controlling the city", She said.

"Well, they probably did that already", Mark said.

"Well we don't have much time left", Marcia said. "Let's get to Triad City and try to stop Dr. Splatter and Dr. Miles before it get worse", She said.

So the kids left the crumble laboratory that was destroy by the Humbugizer's explosion and on their way to Triad City to stop Dr. Splatter and Dr. Miles from taking control of the city.

One hour later, the kids have arrived in Triad City. They had to walk twenty-five miles to get to the city. When they arrive, the city was full of files and bees flying around the city. The Humasects are walking all over the city.

"What happened?" asked Pam, walking towards the city.

"Triad City is a mess", Bobby said.

"This is all Splatter's fault", Mark said.

"What are we going to do?" Pam asked.

"We have to find Dr. Splatter and Dr. Miles and stop this right now", Marcia said.

"Hey looks what I found", Bobby said.

Bobby found a sign at the middle of the street.

"WELCOME TO ENTOMOVILLE", said Pam, reading the sign.

"They have made Triad City as their own", Mark said.

"I think that was his plan all along", Marcia said. "But first we have to find out is the mayor is still alive", She said.

"Good idea Marcia, let's split up and find the mayor and Dr. Splatter and Dr. Miles", Bobby said.

So Marcia and her friends split up and search to find the mayor and the two scientists.

Marcia is searching in the library. The only thing she can find is books and tables on the floor.

"This is a creepy library", said Marcia, walking around the library.

Suddenly a loud broken window was heard in the library.

"What's that? Marcia wondered, looking around the library.

A Humasect jumps in the library and started to chase Marcia in the library.

"Somebody, help me", Marcia yelled, running to escape the Humasect.

Marcia quickly turns around and grabs a wooden chair and hit the Humasect on his head. The wooden chair did not faze the Humasect. Instead, the wooden chair made the Humasect even angrier.

"Now what", She said.

The Humasect opens his mouth and bees and wasps came out of his mouth. Marcia covers her face with her arms and ran out of the library. She hides under a bench right next to a bus stop while the Humasect looks around to find Marcia but the Humascect could not find Marcia. So the Humasect walks away and Marcia came out under the bench and continues her search.

Meanwhile, Pam is searching in the park.

"Sure is dark in here", said Pam, walking in the park. "There is nothing here but flies flying everywhere", She said.

Suddenly, three Humasects lurk in the shadows behind Pam.

"Oh my god, it's those things again", shouted Pam, turns around to see the three Humasects behind her.

Pam quickly turns around the other way and starts running from the Humasects.

"HELP! Pam yelled.

But Pam realizes that she has to face her fears. So Pam turns around and saw the three Humasects. She picks up a solid brick and threw it at one of the Humasects. The solid brick did not faze the Humasect. So Pam ran out of the park and escapes the Humasects.

Meanwhile in a baseball stadium, Mark looks around to find Dr. Splatter and Dr. Miles. The stadium is very quiet. There was no one around. Suddenly something files over Mark's head.

"What was that?" Mark shouted.

Mark look in the sky and saw a giant wasp flying above him.

Oh my God, this wasp is so big", He shouted. "But why this wasp looks like a lady", He wondered.

The giant wasp is no other than Ms. Parks the mayor assistant. So the giant wasp charge Mark with her giant needle. Mark roll out of the way for safely.

"Man, I need a weapon fast", Mark said.

Mark starts running from the giant wasp and try to find a weapon to use. The giant wasp chases Mark around the stadium and Mark running from the wasp. He quickly went to a locker room and closes the door and the giant wasp fly pass the locker room. Mark searches the locker room to find a weapon to use against the wasp. A few minutes later, he found a wooden bat behind the table.

"Nice, this will work just fine", He said. "Now you big fat creature, you are going to get it.

Mark went out of the locker room and enters the field. He found the giant wasp flying around the stadium.

"Hey stingy, come and get some", Mark shouted, holding the bat like he about to take a swing.

The giant wasp charge Mark with her giant needle and Mark roll out of the way. Mark quickly swings the bat at the giant wasp and knocks the giant wasp out of the sky. While the wasp is on the ground, Mark repeatedly beats the wasp with the bat until the wasp was crush into pieces.

"Oh my God, I'm glad that's over with", He said.

Mark walks out of the stadium with his bat and continue his search to find the scientists.

Bobby arrives at the mayor's office to find the mayor. What he found was a lot of papers on the ground, tables and desks torn to pieces on the ground, and a lot of blood on the ground.

"WOW! What happen here?" Bobby wondered.

Suddenly a moan sound was coming from a closet.

"Who's there?" He asked.

Bobby tiptoes to the closet and open the door slowly. The unknown person jumps out of the closet and landed on the floor.

"Oh my God, it's the mayor", Bobby said.

"Helpppppp meeeeeeee", Mayor Jones said, holding his wound ribs.

"What happen to you Mayor Jones?" Bobby asked.

"There were two scientists with weird monsters destroy the office and took the key to the city", Mayor Jones said. "Plus they attack my secretary and took her", He said.

"Don't worry Mayor Jones, me and my friends will stop Dr. Splatter and Dr. Miles from taken over the city", Bobby said. "Do you know where they're at?" He asked.

"I heard them talking and saying that they will work on their experiments at Triad……..Palace", Mayor Jones said.

Suddenly Mayor Jones starts too changed. The mayor was crying in pain. His heart was pumping faster and faster. He was shaking like he was having a seizure.

"What's wrong with you Mayor", asked Bobby, yelling with fear.

"It must be that needle one of the scientists struck me", Mayor Jones said. "I think it has affect……" The Mayor just died.

"Mayor…….Mayor…….MAYORRRRRRR", Bobby shouted.

Bobby begins to walk away and leave the mayor's

office. A minute later, a giant moth burst out of the mayor's stomach.

"What in the world?" Bobby shouted. "I have to get out of here and warn the others", He said.

So Bobby ran out of the mayor's office to find his friends. The giant moth flew out of the office and begins to chase Bobby.

CHAPTER 9

Search for Triad Palace

Inside Triad Palace, Dr. Splatter and Dr. Miles are planning a big plan to take over the world.

"I can't wait until we take over the world", Dr. Splatter said.

"But how are we going to change everyone into Humasects", Dr. Miles said.

"Well, I will built a special laser and place it on top of the satellite in the universe and once it strikes at anyone in the city, it will change them to a Humasect", Dr. Splatter said. "Then, we will be the new masters of this planet", He said.

"I see, well I think we should get started on building this laser", Dr. Miles said.

While Dr. Splatter and Dr. Miles are building the laser to change everyone into Humasects, Marcia, Mark, and Pam are waiting for Bobby at the middle of Entomoville.

"Where is Bobby? asked Pam, standing in the middle of the street. "What's taking him so long?" She said.

"Bobby is probably gone to the book store to steal some books", Mark said.

"Bobby will never steal anything", Marcia said.

"He stole your pencils once", Mark said.

"You're lying", Marcia said.

"Guys, this is serious", Pam said. "Bobby could be lost or something worse in this terrible place", She said.

The kids waited for Bobby for ten minutes. Entomoville was very quiet and very windy.

Ten minutes later, Bobby had finally showed up.

"Hey guys!" Bobby shouted, running in the streets.

"Hey look its Bobby", Marcia shouted.

"Where have you been?" Mark asked.

"I went to the mayor's office to find the mayor", Bobby said.

"Where is the mayor?" Pam asked.

"The mayor is dead", Bobby said.

"You kidding", Marcia said.

"No it's true", Bobby said. "A giant moth bust out of his stomach", He said.

"No way", Mark said.

"What are we going to do now?" Pam asked.

"Before the mayor had changed, he says that Dr. Splatter and Dr. Miles went to Triad Palace", Bobby said.

"Where is Triad Palace?" Marcia asked.

"I don't know", Bobby said.

"We have to find Triad Palace and stop Dr. Splatter and Dr. Miles before they take over the world", Pam said.

"Agree, let's go", Marcia said.

But before they began their search to find Triad Palace, the giant moth swoops down across the kids.

"Look, there is that giant moth that I was talking about", Bobby shouted.

"Wow! That moth is huge", Mark said.

The giant moth files over the kids and begin to spread pollen all over them.

"Cover your eyes, this pollen could be poison", said Marcia, covering her face.

The kids roll out of the way to dodge the pollen from the giant moth.

"How are we going to kill this giant moth?" Pam asked.

Bobby looks around to find a plan to kill the giant moth.

"I GOT IT", Bobby shouted.

Bobby grabs a pole from the ground, runs behind the giant moth and roll to a fire hydrant.

"We have to make the moth chase us to the fire hydrant", said Bobby, standing right beside the fire hydrant.

"All right, we have to do it", Marcia said.

"Ok, let's go", Mark said.

Marcia, Pam, and Mark begin to run towards the fire hydrant. The giant moth turns around and begins to chase the kids. Marcia, Pam, and Mark were running fast as they can to run away from the giant moth and make him get close to Bobby. The giant moth was flying fast as he can but the giant moth could not keep up with the kids. Instead, the giant moth opens his mouth and spit out little baby moths. The baby moths are faster than the giant moth and the baby moths caught up with the kids. One of the baby moths went close to Mark and went inside his arm.

"Ah! my arm", shouted Mark, holding his arm.

"Mark, don't stop running", Pam said.

"This moth is inside my arm", Mark shouted. "I can't control my arm", He said.

Marcia and Pam stop running and saw Mark holding his arm.

"Hang on Mark", Marcia said.

The baby moth that was inside of Mark's arm floating around his body and bust out through his right leg to escape.

"AH MY LEG", Mark yelled, holding his right leg.

The baby moth bust out of Mark's right leg and made a small hole in his leg.

"We have to help Mark", Marcia said.

"But how, we can't stop those moths", Pam said.

"But we can't leave Mark alone out there", Marcia said.

"Ok, we have to carry him over to the fire hydrant", Pam said.

So Marcia and Pam run towards Mark to help him.

"Come on Mark, let's go", Marcia said.

Marcia and Pam carry Mark and running from the moths. The moths begin to chase them but Marcia, Pam, and Mark were slowing down. The moths were getting closer and closer to the kids but Pam had stopped.

"Pam, what are you doing?" Marcia asked.

Pam had let go of Mark and turns around.

"You moths will not eat us alive", Pam said.

Pam took off her shirt and swing at the baby moths. The baby moths were down.

"COME ON", Marcia shouted.

Marcia and Pam carry Mark once again and continue to run towards the fire hydrant but the giant moth begins to chase them again. They finally reach the fire hydrant safely and stand behind Bobby. The giant moth was running towards the kids and Bobby hit the fire hydrant with the pole and water swoosh out of the fire hydrant and hit the giant moth. The giant moth slowly landed on the ground and did not move.

Meanwhile in Triad Palace, Dr. Splatter and his assistant Dr. Miles just completed their special laser to change everyone into a Humasect.

"Yes, it is finally completed", Dr. Splatter said.

"I can't wait to take over the world", Dr. Miles said.

"I will call this laser HUMASECT 3000", Dr. Splatter said. "Again, I will place the Humasect 3000 on top of the satellite and then we will begin our plan", He said.

"But we need a space shuttle to travel to space", Dr. Miles said.

"Yes of course, this is step one of our plan", Dr. Splatter said.

"Well what are we waiting for?" Dr. Miles asked. "Let's do this", He said.

So Dr. Splatter and Dr. Miles left Triad Palace to find a space shuttle. Meanwhile in the streets of Entomoville, Marcia and her friends were still walking to search for Triad Palace after they kill the giant moth. The kids are walking down the street slowly and Mark is still injured from the moth. The right leg that the moth burst out from is cover up by a tee shirt that Mark used from his body. While they were walking down the street, they walk towards a library.

"Hey, let's go to the library and find Triad Palace", Bobby said.

"Hey, that's a great idea", Marcia said.

"I am getting tired of going to the library", Mark said.

"Come on, let's go, Pam said.

So the kids went to the library to find Triad Palace. They did a lot of research to find Triad Palace. Until thirty minutes later, they found it.

"Oh here it is, Triad Palace is locate in the state capital on 29th street", Marcia said.

"That's only ten miles away", Pam said.

"Well, we have to walk over there unless we can find a car or some bikes to get there", Bobby said.

"Well, I guess we have to walk over there", Marcia said.

"All right, let's go", Mark said.

So Marcia and her friends left the library and walk to Triad Palace. Meanwhile back in the front of Triad Palace, Dr. Splatter and Dr. Miles is still working on their evil plan.

"How are we going to find a space shuttle?" Dr. Miles asked.

"Easy Dr. Miles, we have to take a plane to Columbia and steal a space shuttle", Dr. Splatter said.

"This should be a piece of cake" Dr. Miles said. "But, do you know how to fly a plane Dr. Splatter?" Dr. Miles asked.

"Yes of course, I took flying lessons when I was a kid", Dr. Splatter said.

"Oh it's really should be a piece of cake", Dr. Miles said.

"Come on, we have to go to the airport and take the plane to Columbia", Dr. Splatter said.

So Dr. Splatter and Dr. Miles left Triad Palace and on their way to the airport. They took the Humasect 3000 with them and carry it. Meanwhile back in the streets, Marcia and her friends are walking to find Triad Palace.

"STOP!" Marcia shouted. "Look over there", She said.

Marcia saw Triad Palace and they were three miles away.

"Is that Triad Palace?" Pam asked.

"It seems like it and I can't believe it", Bobby said.

Come on, we have to keep moving", Mark said.

"Yes, we have to find Dr. Splatter and Dr. Miles before they take over the world", Marcia said.

So the kids continue to walk towards Triad Palace. When they got there, they spotted Dr. Splatter and Dr. Miles walking towards the kids.

"Oh my God, it's them", Marcia said.

"Quick hide", Bobby said.

The kids hide behind the bench next to the bus stop.

"What are they doing?" Pam asked.

"I guess they are planning their plan to take over the world", Marcia said.

"The airport should be ten miles away", Dr. Splatter said, walking past the kids who were behind the bench.

"They are going to an airport", Pam whispered.

"I wonder what they are planning to do at the airport", Marcia whispered.

"I say we attack them from behind", Mark whispered.

"Good idea Mark", Bobby whispered.

"All right, me and Bobby attack Dr. Splatter from behind while you two attack Dr. Miles from behind", Marcia whispered

"Ok, on my count 1…..2……3", Bobby whispered.

Marcia and her friends run towards Dr. Splatter and Dr. Miles from behind.

"CHARGEEEEEEEE" the kids shouted.

The kids grab Dr. Splatter and Dr. Miles and tie them up with their tee shirts.

"What is the meaning of this?" asked Dr. Splatter, who is tie up.

"You know what's going on", Marcia said. "We are stopping you before you kill anyone else", She said.

"How do you escape the cage?" Dr. Miles asked.

"Easy, we came up with a plan to escape", Bobby said.

"You stupid kids will not get away with this", Dr. Miles said.

"Oh we will", Mark said.

"Come on guys, let's take them in a safe place", Marcia said.

"Hey, what are we going to do about this thing?" Bobby asked.

Bobby is holding the Humasect 3000 in his hand.

"Well, bring it with us and hopefully we can sell it", Pam said.

"This thing could be dangerous so let's break into pieces and sell it for money", Mark said.

"Yeah, I like that idea", Pam said.

"But where are we taking them?" Bobby asked.

"Let's take them in a shelter", Marcia said.

"Fine, let's go", Mark said.

So Marcia, Mark and Pam drag Dr. Splatter and Dr. Miles in a shelter down the street while Bobby is carrying the laser. Dr. Splatter and Dr. Miles were struggling to break free from the tee shirts.

"I can't believe that we are capture by these stupid kids", Dr. Miles said.

"Oh shut up Miles, I will think of something", Dr. Splatter said.

Dr. Splatter thinks to escape from the kids.

"If I can just........there", Dr. Splatter said, pulling out a knife from his back pocket.

"What are we going to do with these two?" Pam asked.

"We have to report them to the police at a different city", Marcia said.

Suddenly Dr. Splatter used the knife from his back pocket, cut through the shirt and broke free.

"I'm free!" Dr. Splatter said.

Dr. Splatter had gotten free and kicks Bobby to the ground that was holding the laser. The laser fell into the ground and Dr. Splatter quickly grabs it.

"Now take this", Dr. Splatter said.

Dr. Splatter fires the Humasect 3000 at the kids. The laser went straight towards the kids but hit Pam right in her chest.

"NOOOOOOOOOOO!" Marcia shouted.

The laser hit Pam but nothing has happen.

"What just happen?" Dr. Splatter said. "It was supposed to change her into a Humasect", He said.

"This is the end of the line for you Splatter", Bobby said.

Bobby tackles Dr. Splatter and quickly tie him up with another tee shirt from this body.

"That's it I'm getting out of here", Dr. Miles said.

Dr. Miles run fast as he can to escape the kids.

"Oh no, he's getting away", Marcia said.

"Oh great, he's gone", Mark said.

"Oh well, don't worry we have the smart one", Marcia said.

"But Dr. Miles can still take over the world", Mark said.

"Ha, he does not have the proper equipment to do that", Dr. Splatter said.

"Be quiet", Marcia said.

"Ughhhhhhhhhh!" Pam moaned.

"What's wrong Pam?" Mark asked.

"We have to get to the shelter quickly", Bobby said.

"Come on, let's go", Marcia said.

Bobby and Marcia drag Dr. Splatter down the street to the shelter while Mark is carrying Pam in his arms.

CHAPTER 10

Pam the Humasect

"I can not believe that we was caught by some high school kids", said Dr. Miles, walking towards Maroon Airlines. "Hmm, I think I go to Paris and take over their city", He said. "But first, I will use them to destroy Trojan City and I will have the knowledge to use Humasects to take over Paris", He said. Dr. Miles went to the airplane and took off and now leaving Trojan City and Entomoville.

Meanwhile in the shelter, Marcia, Bobby, and Mark were finding a cure for Pam while Dr. Splatter is sitting down on the floor tie up.

"Here take this", said Marcia, giving Pam aspirins for her cure.

"Did it work?" Bobby asked.

"Of course it works", Mark said. "Aspirins can cure anything", He said.

Pam is resting on the floor feeling her head.

"Ugh!" Pam moaned.

"Listen to her, she's changing", Dr. Splatter said.

"Shut up Splatter!" said Mark, smacking Dr. Splatter in the face. "It's your fault she's like this", He said.

"Pam you need to relax a little bit", Marcia said.

"There is nothing you can do to save her", Dr. Splatter said. "In a few minutes your friend is going to turn into a Humasect", He said.

"Shut up Splatter!" said Mark, smacking Dr. Splatter in the face.

"There got to be something that we can use to save her", Bobby said.

"You can't do anything you stupid kids", Dr. Splatter said.

Mark took his right shoe off and took off his sock and put his sock on Splatter's mouth.

"Here eat this", Mark said.

"Let's just go to sleep and relax", Bobby said.

"I can't relax in a situation like this", Mark said. "We need to find a cure before Pam turns into these creatures and we don't want to face another monster", He said.

"Well I'm going to sleep", Marcia said.

"Me too", Bobby said.

"Alright, I guess I go to sleep as well", Mark said. "But we must find a cure first thing in the morning", He said.

"Agree!" Marcia said.

So Marcia, Bobby, and Mark begin to fall asleep. They will try to find a cure first thing in the morning.

One hour later, Pam woke up and went to the ladies washroom.

"I can't go to sleep", Pam said to herself.

Pam looks in the mirror and sees her face begins to change.

"Ugh, what's happening to me?" She said. "I can't take this anymore and I wish I can kill Dr. Splatter but he probably got the cure", She said.

Suddenly, Pam's stomach begins to growl.

"Ahhhhhh! It hurts", Pam shouted, holding her stomach.

"Guys wake up", Marcia shouted to Mark and Bobby. "Pam is started to change", She said.

"Oh yes, she is changing into a Humasect and there is nothing you can do about it", Dr. Splatter said. "She will be under my control", He said.

"Pam snap out of it", Marcia said.

"Don't let Splatter get to you", Mark said.

"I can't control it", Pam said.

Pam is beginning to grow longer teeth and grow extra arms.

"No, it's too late", Marcia said.

"I can't believe she's a Humasect", Mark said.

Pam has longer teeth, four arms, and got wings to fly.

"Look at my creation", Dr. Splatter said. "Pam has become a Super Humasect", He said.

We have to find a cure fast", Marcia said.

"It's too late you stupid kids" Dr. Splatter said. "She is now under my control", He said.

"There is nothing we can do", Bobby said.

"Now my pet, kill your pretty friends", Dr. Splatter shouted.

"Come on Pam, we're your friends", Marcia said.

Pam who is now a Humasect walk towards her friends and suddenly stopped. She looks at them with her red furious eyes.

"Please Pam snap out of it", Marcia said.

Pam turns around and looks at Dr. Splatter.

"What are you looking at you stupid girl?" Dr. Splatter asked. "Kill those precious little friends of your", He said.

The Humasect Pam opens her mouth and bees and wasps came out and attack Dr. Splatter.

"Ahhhhh, get these things off me", Dr. Splatter shouted.

"Yeah that's it Pam, get him", Marcia said.

The bees and wasps was eating and stinging Dr. Splatter's face while he was still tie up.

"Ughhhhhhh!" Pam growled.

"Pam calm down, we are here to help you", Marcia said.

"Don't do anything crazy", Bobby said.

Pam slowly turns around and saw her friends. She ran towards them, stab Mark right in his stomach, and slice his whole body in half.

"Noooooooooo!" Marcia cried.

"She killed Mark", Bobby said.

I must stop her now before one of us gets killed by her", Marcia said.

"What are we going to do?" Bobby asked.

"We have to kill our friend", Marcia said.

"Are you crazy?" Bobby asked.

"Bobby, we have no other choice but to killed her", Marcia said.

"Ok, we need to find a good weapon to used", Bobby said.

"All right, I find a good weapon to use on her while you distract her", Marcia said.

"Ok, let's do it", Bobby said.

So Marcia tries to find a weapon to use on Pam while Bobby distracts her.

"Hey Pam over here", Bobby said to Pam.

Pam starts to chase Bobby with her enormous speed. Suddenly Marcia found a wooden stick under a big desk.

All right, this will work", Marcia said. "Hey, I found a good weapon", She said. "Hey Bobby, make her run towards me", She said.

Bobby runs towards Marcia while Pam runs and follows him. Bobby hides behind Marcia and Marcia hit Pam with the wooden stick on her head and knocks her to the ground.

"You force me to do it Pam", Marcia said. "You killed Mark and you have to pay for it", She said.

But it wasn't over yet. Pam quickly gets up and slice Marcia on her left leg with her claws.

"Ahhhhhh, she's not dead", cried Marcia, holding her left leg.

"We have to find something powerful than a wooden stick", Bobby said.

So Bobby quickly runs towards the desk to find something else.

"Hurry!" Marcia cried, while Pam walking towards Marcia.

Suddenly Bobby found a gun on one of the drawers in the desk. Bobby grabs the gun and shot Pam on her head and her head explodes. Pam's body falls down.

"Thank God, it's over", Marcia said.

"Are you okay Marcia?" Bobby asked.

"Yeah, I think I can still walk", Marcia said.

"Ok, we need to get out of this city", Bobby said.

"That's a good idea" Marcia said. "Come on, let's get out of here", She said.

"Don't leave me here", Dr. Splatter said, on the ground while the bees and wasps still buzzing around him.

"Let him be, he deserves to laid there", Marcia said.

So Marcia and Bobby left the shelter to find a way to get out of the city.

Ten minutes has passed and a Humasect walks in the shelter. He saw Dr. Splatter tie up and be eaten and stung by the bees and wasps. So the Humasect suck all of the bees and wasps around Dr. Splatter with his mouth, cut the tee shirts with his claws and save Dr. Splatter.

"Thank you my Humasect", Dr. Splatter said, while the Humasect cutting him loose. "Those stupid kids will not escape me", He said.

CHAPTER 11

Escaping the Nightmare

"Where's the airport"? Bobby asked.

"It's somewhere outside the city", Marcia said.

The kids are running to escape Entomoville and tried to find the airport.

"We need to find a car for crying out loud", Bobby said.

"Yes, I am getting tired of running", said Marcia, while trying to catch her breath.

The kids had stop running to search for a car.

"Do you know how to drive Bobby?" Marcia asked.

"Well just a little bit", Bobby said. "My mother taught me how to drive three years ago", He said.

"Good, all we need is to find a car", Marcia said.

"But where can we find a good car?" Bobby asked.

"We may have to find one in one of those car shops", Marcia said.

"Good idea!" Bobby said. "Ok let's do it", He said.

So Marcia and Bobby begin to search for a car shop

so they can find a car to drive to the airport and escape Entomoville.

Meanwhile Dr. Splatter had just leaving the shelter with the Humasect.

"It's time to create my greatest creature THE HUMABEE", Dr. Splatter said. "Hey Humasect, spit out a bee for me", He said.

So the Humasect spit out a bee from his mouth and then grabs it and kills it.

"Alright, I will use this bee and fuse with a Humasect to create the most powerful creature in the universe HA…..HA…..HA", Dr. Splatter laughing with anger.

So Dr. Splatter took a blood sample from the bee, mix it with a special acid from his bottle, put it inside the needle, and stab the Humasect with the needle. One minute later, the Humasect screams in pain and suddenly the Humasect begins to grow some wings in his back. His legs were automatic cut off from his body and a hornet came out of his body. The Humasect had change into a Humabee.

"Yes….Yes…..Yes", Dr. Splatter shouted. "My creation is finally completed and now let's find those stupid teenagers and kill them before they escaped", He said.

The Humabee left Dr. Splatter and begin to search for Marcia and Bobby. Meanwhile, Marcia and Bobby found a car at a nearby car shop.

"Hey, what do you think about this car?" Bobby asked.

"No that's too rusty", Marcia said. "Now this is a perfect car", She said.

Marcia had found a 2004 Lexus right next to the other rusty cars.

"Now let's find the keys inside the office", Marcia said.

"OK!" Bobby replied.

So the kids grab the keys from the office, got inside the car and drove away. Bobby is the one driving the car while Marcia is sitting next to him.

While they were driving down the street, a buzzing noise was heard.

"Hey, did you hear that?" Bobby asked.

"Who cares, it's probably bees flying around", Marcia said.

"Maybe you're right", Bobby said.

Then another loud buzzing sound was heard.

"Hey, that's no ordinary buzz from a bee", Bobby said.

"Don't worry about it, just keep driving", Marcia said.

Suddenly the Humabee smash through the passenger side of the car.

"Oh my God, what is that?" Bobby yelled.

"It looks like a half Humasect half bee", Marcia said. "Come on, we have to get out of here", She said.

Bobby puts the car in drive and drove away from the Humabee. The Humabee starts chasing Marcia and Bobby with his enormous speed. The Humabee go in front of the car and smash the windshield. The Humabee opens his right hand and shot bees through his hands.

"Ah, get these creatures off me", Marcia yelled.

Bobby puts the car in reverse to escape the Humabee and the bees that were attacking them. He made a U-turn to go the other direction but the Humabee was too fast for them. The Humabee got in front of them and the kids ran over the Humabee. The Humabee flew across the ground and landed on his back. The kids were fine but the Humabee was not. The kids got out of the car to check on the Humabee.

"Aw man, I think the monster is dead", said Bobby, looking at the Humabee from outside.

"Well, the car is in bad shape", Marcia said.

"Well, I guess we have to walk to the airport now", Bobby said.

So Marcia and Bobby left the damage car and start walking and head towards the airport. Suddenly the Humabee got up off the ground and starts flying towards the kids.

"Wait a minute, he's still alive", Bobby said. Bobby turns around and saw the Humabee flying towards them.

"What are we going to do now Bobby?" Marcia asked.

"We have no choice but to run", Bobby said.

"No, I am getting tired of running", Marcia said. "We must beat this thing right now", She said.

"All right, let's find something powerful to use to beat this creature", Bobby said.

So Marcia and Bobby look around to find something useful to use to defeat the Humabee. The Humabee were getting closer and closer to Marcia and Bobby. Suddenly Bobby found a large pole, which is almost taller than them put together on the ground.

"Hey, let's use this", Bobby said.

"I don't think that's strong enough", Marcia said.

"Sure it is, all we have to do is to stab him with the pole", Bobby said.

"But the pole is not sharp it's shining", Marcia said.

But we can still beat him", Bobby said.

"Alright, let's see what happens", Marcia said.

So Marcia and Bobby grab the pole and run towards the Humabee. The Humabee slice Bobby on his forehead with his claws and bring Bobby to the ground.

"BOBBYYYYY!" Marcia cried.

"I'm okay", said Bobby, getting up from the ground.

"Marcia grabs the large pole with both hands and swings the pole as fast as she and knock the Humabee off the ground. Bobby got up off the ground, took the pole from Marcia with anger, and swings the pole as fast as he can and slam the pole on the Humabee while the creature was on the ground. Bobby repeatedly slams the pole on the ground hitting the creature on top of his head. The Humabee was busted it wide open and there was blood all over his face. Bobby once again hit the creature in his head with the large pole and knocks the Humabee's head off of his body.

"Oh my God, that's the end of that chapter", Marcia said.

"Yeah, I hope he doesn't come back", Bobby said.

"C'mon, we have to get on an airplane and fly out of here", Marcia said.

"Who's going to fly the plane?" Bobby asked.

"Well I guess I have to fly the plane", Marcia said.

"Do you know how to fly a plane?" Bobby asked.

"Well in the time like this, I don't have a choice", Marcia said.

"Marcia, let's get out of here together and start a new life together", Bobby said.

"Oh Bobby, I was scare of telling you how much I feel about you", Marcia said. "I was dreaming about us getting married and have two beautiful children of our own", She said.

"We're almost there Marcia", Bobby said.

Bobby holds Marcia hands and gave her a kiss.

Come on Marcia, let's get out of here", He said.

Bobby and Marcia start walking once again and headed towards the airport.

CHAPTER 12

Trojan City and Entomoville's Destruction

Dr. Splatter is walking down the streets to find the Humabee and the kids.

"Where is my creation?" Dr. Splatter asked. "I wonder my Humabee kill those crazy teenagers", He said.

Dr. Splatter is walking in the streets and come across a huge mess right next to the car shop.

"I wonder what happen here", He wondered. "I smell human blood and it smells like my Humabee did an excellent job taking care of those teenagers", He said. "But I don't see anything and where are their dead bodies?" He asked to himself.

Dr. Splatter is looking around the car shop to see if Bobby and Marcia dead.

"Hey, what is that?" He asked. Dr. Splatter has found his Humabee's head on the ground and the rest of his body right next to him.

"What happen to you?" He asked, looking at the Humabee. "Those teenagers will pay for this", He said. "They force me to create the most powerful Humasect in the world and it may kill me", He said.

So Dr. Splatter took all of the dead insects from the ground and took all of their blood, took a blood sample from the dead Humabee and mixes it in his bottle and drinks it.

"I hope this works otherwise it's going to kill me", He said.

Ten minutes later, Dr. Splatter's heart starts to pump really fast.

"Ugh, this is it, it seems that I'm changing", He said.

Dr. Splatter was on the ground holding his chest.

"Oh my God, this pain is enormous", He said. "I can't take this anymore", He said.

Suddenly Dr. Splatter starts to grow longer teeth. His eyes begin to turn green. His arms begin to turn into long claws. Dr. Splatter has long wings bigger than a single fly. He has change into the ultimate Humasect in the universe.

"Yes….Yes….Yes, I feel so great", He said. "I can't wait until I find those teenagers", He said.

Dr. Splatter flies into the sky to search for Bobby and Marcia. He can hear and see over 100 feet far away with his eyes and ears.

"Ha, I can see them", He said. "I see that they going to the airport but whose going to fly the plane, everyone is dead", He said. "I have to stop them".

So Dr. Splatter flies towards Marcia and Bobby with his super speed and got right in front of them.

"Oh my goodness, is that Splatter?" Bobby asked.

"Oh no, we was so close to the airport", Marcia said.

"Sorry kiddies, I can not allow you to go any further", Dr. Splatter said. "You stupid kids ruin everything and now you are going to pay for it", He said.

"That creature was no match for us", Marcia said.

"Yeah, we destroy that creature with a car and a pole", Bobby said.

"WHAT?" Dr. Splatter shouted.

"If we did that to your monster then we can do the same to you", Marcia said.

"Oh I see, well the important thing is I'm still alive and there is nothing you kids can do about it", Dr. Splatter said.

"Well Splatter, it's two against one", Bobby said. "What are you going to do about it", He said.

"It's simple, I'm going to destroy you both", Dr. Splatter said. "COME AND GET THEM", He shouted.

"You ready Bobby", Marcia said.

"Yeah, let's do this", Bobby said.

Marcia and Bobby charge Dr. Splatter with their ball up fist and punch Dr. Splatter in his stomach but did not hurt him.

"Ha, that's all you got", Dr. Splatter said.

Dr. Splatter slashes both Marcia and Bobby with his claws and Marcia and Bobby falls onto the ground.

"Are you okay Marcia?" Bobby asked, slowly gets up from the ground.

"Yeah let's just go for the face", Marcia said.

Marcia and Bobby charge Dr. Splatter with deadly uppercuts in the face. But Dr. Splatter stares at them with his green eyes and slash them again with his claws.

"C'mon kids, you can do better than that", Dr. Splatter said.

"All right, let's go for the legs", Marcia said.

"Right" Bobby responds.

Marcia and Bobby try to trip Dr. Splatter both legs but it was hopeless. Dr. Splatter did not go down and Marcia and Bobby step back.

"You can't beat me", Dr. Splatter said. "I am invincible", He said.

"Do you have any other plans Bobby?" Marcia asked.

"No, I'm out of ideas", Bobby said.

"Well, I guess I have to finish you off", Dr. Splatter said.

Dr. Splatter starts charging with his claws and stab Bobby through his stomach.

"BOBBBBBYYYYYYY!" Marcia shouted.

Dr. Splatter picks up Bobby with his claw and threw him in the ground.

"You monster how could you?" Marcia asked.

Marcia ran towards Bobby and covers his wounded with her tee shirt.

"Bobby, are you alright?" Marcia asked.

"Marcia, I can't hold on much longer", Bobby said silently.

"Bobby just hold on and rest here for a minute", Marcia said.

"Marcia, I always loves you from the day I met you", Bobby said. "One day, I wanted us to be together, get married someday, and start a new life together", He said.

"I......" Bobby just passed out in Marcia arms.

"Bobby…..Bobby…..BOBBYYYYYYY", Marcia cried.

Bobby couldn't hold on and just died in Marcia's arms.

"Oh how touching, it looks like a drama movie", Dr. Splatter said.

Marcia place Bobby on the ground and cover his eyes. Marcia wipes her tears, quickly turns around and looks at Dr. Splatter straight in his eyes.

"You will pay for this Splatter", Marcia said with anger.

"What are you going to do little girl?" Dr. Splatter said. "I'm in invincible", He said.

"But why did you turn Trojan City into a hive?" Marcia asked.

"It's simple, let me tell you a story", Dr. Splatter said.

"Five years ago, I was one of the top entomologists in this city. I have created flying spiders as my first set of creatures. Then, I was hired at Pesticide Corporation to create something that was unbelievable than any other flying insects. I had an idea with humans and insects and I say to myself what if humans and insects were fuse together. That will be the greatest

insect that I ever created. So I begin to jot down ideas of how I'm going to create this. Then it hit me, just takes a blood sample from any insect and transfers it with a human body. So I asked one of the scientists from Pesticide Corporation to be my test subject and he agrees of becoming one of the greatest creatures in the whole galaxy. So I took dead insects, took a blood sample from his body and mix it together and let him drink it. After ten minutes, he was beginning to change. He has long claws, long teeth, huge wings, and make bugs comes out in his mouth. After that, I had the idea of calling this powerful creature "HUMASECT". Pretty much, that's when I decided to take over and become the most powerful entomologist in the universe".

"So you see, this is like an insect world built with enormous creatures throughout the galaxy and the city has a new mayor now and his name is Dr. Joe Splatter, the most powerful and the top entomologists in the galaxy", He said.

"That I'm going to killed", Marcia said.

"And how are you going to do that little girl", Dr. Splatter asked.

"I'm going to knock you out", Marcia replied.

Marcia run towards Dr. Splatter and charge him with a fierce punch on his face.

"Is that all you got little girl?" Dr. Splatter asked. "Your fist does not hurt me", He said.

Marcia had back away from Dr. Splatter and think of another plan to kill Dr. Splatter.

"This guy is really tough", Marcia said. "There is no other way to beat him", She said.

Suddenly a loud noise is roaring from the sky. A helicopter swoosh pass Marcia and Dr. Splatter.

"Hey you down there step away from the monster", Officer Francis Winkfield said.

"Please help me!" Marcia shouted.

"Stay out of my way", Dr. Splatter shouted.

Dr. Splatter blast wasps and bees through his hands at the helicopter and helicopter went out of control. The helicopter crash to the ground and the officer and the driver had jump out of the helicopter.

"Oh great, how I'm supposed to escape this time?" Marcia asked to herself.

"Oh I'm sorry, was that your way to escaped", Dr. Splatter asked.

"What to do now?" Marcia asked. "Hey, what's that?" She said silently.

Marcia found a rocket launcher behind Dr. Splatter.

"I wonder it came from the helicopter", She said. "This might be my ticket out of here", She said.

"Well I guess it's time to destroy you", Dr. Splatter said.

"Well then, come and get me you Humasect", Marcia said.

Dr. Splatter run towards Marcia and tries to slash her with her claws but Marcia rolls out of the way and run towards the rocket launcher.

"Hey Splatter, YOU'RE FINISHED", Marcia shouted.

Marcia pulls the trigger and the rocket fires towards Dr. Splatter and Dr. Splatter had exploded into million pieces.

"Oh my God, that's the end of the nightmare", Marcia said.

Marcia was lying on the ground to catch her breath.

"Hey little girl, we have to get out of here", Officer Francis Winkfield said. "Bombs are already been place all around the city", He said.

"Who sent you here?" Marcia asked.

"Our Mayor sent us to destroy Trojan City because a scientist came from here and told us that the city was taking over by insects", Officer Francis Winkfield said. "The Mayor filed a report to the President and the President gave us the okay to send our troops to destroy this city", He said.

"Wait, what scientist?" Marcia asked.

"I heard his name was Dr. Miles", Officer Francis Winkfield said.

"WHAT? Marcia shouted. "Your mayor is crazy", She said.

"I beg your pardon", Officer Winkfield said.

"If you don't know, Dr. Miles is Dr. Splatter assistant", Marcia said.

"Ok, who is Dr. Splatter?" Officer Winkfield asked.

"That's the monster that I just killed with the rocket launcher", Marcia said. "There is a possibility that Dr. Miles is going to take over your city pretty soon", She said.

"Oh I see, well we have to call in another helicopter since the one that was crash is in pretty bad shape", Officer Winkfield said. "It may take couple of hours", He said.

"Well how long do we have until the bombs goes off?" Marcia asked.

"The bombs have been set for two hours", Officer Winkfield said.

"Well we have to hide until the helicopter gets here otherwise the Humasects will smell and find us", Marcia said.

"Where are we going to hide?" Officer Winkfield asked.

"Let's hide in that store over there", Marcia said.

Marcia pointed at a grocery store across the street from them.

"Ok, let me call for another helicopter", Officer Winkfield said. "Mayday I need another helicopter immediately, do you copy over", He said, talking to his walkie-talkie.

"I hear you loud and clear", Officer Butler respond. "We will come and rescue you ASAP", He said.

"Ok, let's go", Officer Winkfield said. "Come on Steve, we have to move", He said to Steve, who was the driver of the helicopter.

So Marcia, Steve, and Officer Winkfield run towards the store. Officer Winkfield found a brick on the ground and bust the window to get inside the store. They have waited and waited for the helicopter. Inside the store, they have food to eat and water to drink.

Two hours later, the helicopter has arrived.

"Alright, we have to go", Officer Winkfield said.

"Wait, where is the helicopter taken us?" Marcia asked.

"The helicopter will take us to Paris where we will be safe", Officer Winkfield said.

"What are you going to do with me?" Marcia asked.

"Well, we will find you a new home and begin your new life", Officer Winkfield said.

"Ok well I hope I can find me a good home", Marcia said. "Plus, we have to hurry before Dr. Miles do something to your city", She said.

"Well, nothing has happen yet so maybe he does not want to destroy the city", Officer Winkfield said.

"Don't underestimate him", Marcia said. "Let's just find him and see what he is planning", She said.

"Ok, let's just hurry up and get out of here before we turn into dust", Officer Winkfield said.

So Marcia and the officer took off in the helicopter and on their way to Paris. Two minutes later while they were in the sky, the bombs exploded and Entomoville that was created by Dr. Splatter burst into flames. Marcia who was the last survivor from her other three friends will begin her new life. New friends and new adventures await her there in Paris.